A Note to Parents and Caregivers:

Read-it! Readers are for children who are just starting on the amazing road to reading. These beautiful books support both the acquisition of reading skills and the love of books.

The PURPLE LEVEL presents basic topics and objects using high frequency words and simple language patterns.

The RED LEVEL presents familiar topics using common words and repeating sentence patterns.

The BLUE LEVEL presents new ideas using a larger vocabulary and varied sentence structure.

The YELLOW LEVEL presents more challenging ideas, a broad vocabulary, and wide variety in sentence structure.

The GREEN LEVEL presents more complex ideas, an extended vocabulary range, and expanded language structures.

The ORANGE LEVEL presents a wide range of ideas and concepts using challenging vocabulary and complex language structures.

When sharing a book with your child, read in short stretches, pausing often to talk about the pictures. Have your child turn the pages and point to the pictures and familiar words. And be sure to reread favorite stories or parts of stories.

There is no right or wrong way to share books with children. Find time to read with your child, and pass on the legacy of literacy.

Adria F. Klein, Ph.D.
Professor Emeritus
California State University
San Bernardino, California

First American edition published in 2005 by
Picture Window Books
5115 Excelsior Boulevard
Suite 232
Minneapolis, MN 55416
877-845-8392
www.picturewindowbooks.com

First published in Great Britain by Franklin Watts, 96 Leonard Street,
London, EC2A 4XD

Printed in the United States of America.

Library of Congress Cataloging-in-Publication Data
Powell, Jillian.
Izzie's idea / written by Jillian Powell ; illustrated by Leonie Shearing.
p. cm. — (Read-it! readers)
Summary: Izzie learns to help with her new baby brother as her parents explain what it
means each time he cries, but when both of her parents run out of ideas, it is up to Izzie to
stop his tears.
ISBN-10: 1-4048-0644-X (hardcover)
[1. Babies—Fiction. 2. Crying—Fiction. 3. Brothers and sisters—Fiction.] I. Shearing,
Leonie, ill. II. Title. III. Series.
PZ7.P87755Iz 2004
[E]—dc22
2004009180

Izzie's Idea

by Jillian Powell
illustrated by Leonie Shearing

Special thanks to our advisers for their expertise:

Adria F. Klein, Ph.D.
Professor Emeritus, California State University
San Bernardino, California

Susan Kesselring, M.A.
Literacy Educator
Rosemount-Apple Valley-Eagan (Minnesota) School District

PICTURE WINDOW BOOKS
Minneapolis, Minnesota

One day, Izzie's mom came back from the hospital. She brought Izzie a new baby brother, Ben.

As soon as Ben got home,
he cried. He cried so loudly
that he made Izzie cry, too!

Soon Izzie stopped crying. But her baby brother Ben cried louder. "He needs to be fed," Mom said.

Izzie stayed while Mom fed her
baby brother. Before long, Ben
stopped crying.

In the afternoon, Ben cried again.
This time, he cried after he ate.
"He needs his diaper changed,"
Dad said.

So Izzie and Dad changed Ben's
diaper. And Ben soon stopped
crying and fell asleep.

In the evening, Ben cried. He whimpered after he ate.

He wailed after his diaper was changed.

"He's tired," Mom said. "He needs to be rocked." So Izzie gently rocked Ben to sleep.

In the morning, Ben cried again.

He squealed after his bottle.

He squalled after his

diaper was changed.

"He needs a bath," Dad said. So
Izzie and Dad gave Ben a bath.
They dried him and dressed him,
and Ben
fell asleep.

In the afternoon, Ben woke up and cried and cried. Dad fed him. Mom changed his diaper. Ben still cried.

Waaaa!

"Maybe he's bored," said Izzie.

She shook the rattle. Ben bawled.

Ben's face was as red as a plum. "Maybe he wants his teddy bear," said Dad. So Izzie gave Ben his teddy bear. Ben howled.

Waaaa!

18

"Maybe he wants a hug,"
said Mom.

So Izzie gave him a hug, but
Ben did not stop crying.

21

Izzie decided she had to cheer Ben up. She made the duck squeak. Ben cried.

Squeak!

22

She played on her drum.

Ben screamed.

23

Izzie did a handstand. Ben howled.

Then Izzie did cartwheels.

"Look, Ben!" she said.

But Ben was too busy crying.

Izzie tried everything, but nothing stopped Ben's crying. Then Izzie had a brilliant idea.

She put on her earmuffs. They
were pink and very fluffy.

27

Izzie couldn't hear Ben's crying now! Peace at last!

She looked so funny that Mom smiled. Then Dad smiled.

And when Ben saw Izzie,
he stopped crying. "Look!
He's smiling!" said Mom.
And Izzie smiled, too.

More *Read-it!* Readers

Bright pictures and fun stories help you practice your reading skills. Look for more books at your level.

Alex and Toolie

Another Pet

The Big Pig

Bliss, Blueberries, and the Butterfly

Camden's Game

Cass the Monkey

Charlie's Tasks

Clever Cat

Flora McQuack

Kyle's Recess

Marconi the Wizard

Peppy, Patch, and the Postman

Peter's Secret

Pets on Vacation

The Princess and the Tower

Theodore the Millipede

The Three Princesses

Tromso the Troll

Willie the Whale

The Zoo Band

Looking for a specific title or level? A complete list of *Read-it!* Readers is available on our Web site:

www.picturewindowbooks.com